A NOTE TO PARENTS

Reading is often considered the most important skill children learn in the primary grades. Much can be done at home to lay the foundation for early reading success.

When they read, children use the following to figure out words: story and picture clues, how a word is used in a sentence, and sound/spelling relationships. The **Hello Reader!** *Phonics Fun* series focuses on sound/spelling relationships through phonics activities. Phonics instruction unlocks the door to understanding sounds and the letters or spelling patterns that represent them.

The **Hello Reader!** *Phonics Fun* series is divided into the following three sets of books, based on important phonic elements:
- **Sci-Fi Phonics**: word families
- **Monster Phonics**: consonants, blends, and digraphs
- **Funny Tale Phonics**: short and long vowels

Learn About Word Families

The Sci-Fi Phonics stories, including *Boom! Zoom!*, feature words that rhyme and contain the same spelling pattern. These books help children become aware of and use common word parts when decoding, or sounding out, new words. After reading the book, you might wish to begin lists of words that belong to the same word family. Your child can use these lists for reading practice or as reference when spelling words.

Enjoy the Activities
- Challenge your child to build words using the letters and word parts provided. Help your child by demonstrating how to sound out new words.
- Match words with pictures to help your child attach meaning to text.
- Become word detectives by identifying story words with the same sound, letter, or spelling pattern.
- Keep the activities game-like and praise your child's efforts.

Develop Fluency

Encourage your child to read these books again and again and again. Each time, set a different purpose for reading.
- Look for rhyming words or words that begin or end with the same sound.
- Suggest to your child that he or she read the book to a friend, family member, or even a pet.

Whatever you do, have fun with the books and instill the joy of reading in your child. It is one of the most important things you can do!

—Wiley Blevins, Reading Specialist
Ed.M., Harvard University

JE PB

To Genevieve
—J.B.S.

To Kay, Doug, & Noah
—J.Z.

Text copyright © 1997 by Judith Bauer Stamper.
Illustrations copyright © 1997 by Jerry Zimmerman.
All rights reserved. Published by Scholastic Inc.
HELLO READER! and CARTWHEEL BOOKS and associated logos
are trademarks and/or registered trademarks of Scholastic Inc.

Library of Congress Cataloging-in-Publication Data

Stamper, Judith Bauer.
    Boom! Zoom! / by Judith Bauer Stamper; illustrated by Jerry Zimmerman;
phonics activities by Wiley Blevins.
        p.   cm.—(Hello reader! Phonics fun. Sci-fi phonics)
    "Rhyming word families."
    "Cartwheel books."
    Summary: Ray blasts off into space, where he crash lands on a strange planet and must escape from an alien being. Includes related phonics activities.
    ISBN 0-590-76264-8
    [1. Outer space—Fiction. 2. Interplanetary voyages—Fiction.
3. Extraterrestrial beings—Fiction. 4. Stories in rhyme.]
I. Zimmerman, Jerry, ill.   II. Blevins, Wiley.   III. Title.   IV. Series.
PZ8.3.S78255Bo   1997
[E]—dc21

97-14515
CIP
AC

10 9 8 7 6 5 4   8 9/9 0/0 01 02

Printed in the U.S.A.   24
First printing, October 1997

4/99 Jng 2.00

BOOM! ZOOM!

by Judith Bauer Stamper
Illustrated by Jerry Zimmerman
Phonics Activities by Wiley Blevins

Hello Reader! Phonics Fun
Sci-Fi Phonics • Rhyming Word Families

SCHOLASTIC INC.
New York   Toronto   London   Auckland   Sydney

Boom! Up goes Ray.

Zoom! He's far away.

Swing! He's right past Mars.

Zing! He's through the stars.

Bump! It's time to land.

Jump! What's that hand?

Ick! What a face!

Quick! Ray must race.

Stop! My name is Zat.

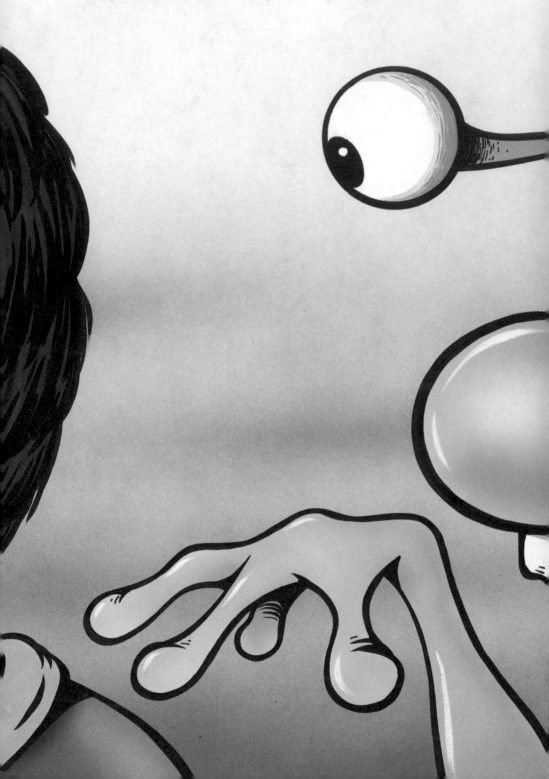

Hop! There's no time to chat.

Run!
Ray's so fast.

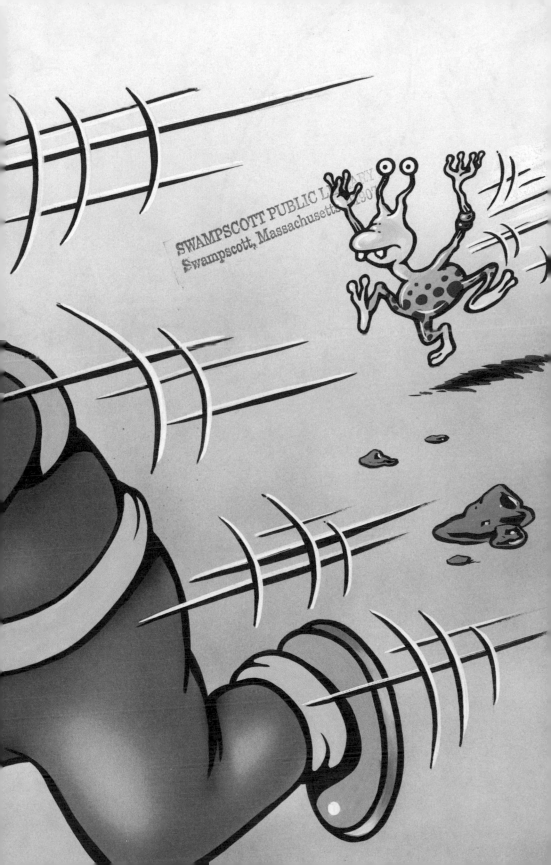

Fun!
It's time to blast.

Pow!
Ray starts the ship.

Wow! What a trip!

• PHONICS ACTIVITIES •
Zat, go home!
Zat must find his way home.
Zat takes the path with objects
whose names end with *at*.

HOME

Picture Match
Find the word in the story that names each picture.

Word Families

Point to the words in each column that belong to the same word family.

B<u>oom</u>	**Qu**<u>ick</u>	**R**<u>ay</u>	**Pl**<u>ace</u>
zoom	lick	day	nice
room	read	say	race
seed	sick	fly	face
broom	pick	pay	space

Answer

Zat, go home!

HOME